Release Me

Release Me

Gearline Young

Library of Congress Control Number: 2021917857
ISBN: Hardcover   978-1-6641-9267-6
                  Softcover   978-1-6641-9266-9
                  eBook   978-1-6641-9265-2

Rev. date: 08/27/2021

To order additional copies of this book, contact:
Xlibris
844-714-8691
www.Xlibris.com
Orders@Xlibris.com
830958

Anxious Ann

Philippians 4:6--7 commanded the Philippians to be "anxious for nothing; but in everything by prayer and supplication, with thanksgiving, let your requests be made known to God; and the peace of God, which surpasses all understanding, will guard your hearts and minds through Christ Jesus."

Ann doubted God when she became obsessed with her plans to rid her mind about her husband's choices. "Being anxious for nothing," did not mean anything to her. Fear appeared, causing a real jolt in the family's daily life, when they decided to move to a strange metropolitan town. She could not cope with her husband's absence from home due to his new career. She began to think thoughts of suspicion about their marriage. Her husband, Greg, did not adjust to the new community; and to make it worst, he began moving from one job to another.

Ann's misgivings grew into anger, causing her to think selfishly about her duties at the home. Greg began to express himself in accusatory outbursts. He became a verbal abuser; that is, scolding without apologies. Why did Ann accept the responsibility for Greg's anger when it was unjustified? Did she feel better making him happy after the abuse? Was she responsible for his happiness? Did she prove her love by agreeing with anything that he wishes? Ann's rage began to slowly disappear when she recognized that she was being verbally abused; she began acting in her own interest. She stopped feeling inadequate; and increased her spirit of acceptance of herself and worth.

When Greg apologized, he did not ask Ann about ways to behave in a more positive manner. He did not seem to show any love to Ann. Instead he increased his abuse by telling her how worthless she was; he even threatened physical pain. She was in an unsafe environment. She had stopped feeling inadequate; but did not want to feel insecure.

Greg lost his last job during the last recession; and Ann began feeling scared. She could not sleep at night and often cried; but she stayed on her knees praying to God. Was her love for Jesus Christ being replaced with her love for Greg? She started to try harder to win Greg's love by letting him control her behavior.

Ann decided to attend church frequently. At least she could pray and participate in activities with Christian friends. She wanted to run away from Greg because he was so rude. He began every day with unkind words to disrespect her. His hostile behavior frightened her. Why was Greg attacking her? She felt hopeless and wanted to give up everything. The kind words of the church members kept her sane. Participation in church activities motivated her to persevere. Christ's love never fails; she prayed with her heart for God to remove these emotions.

Greg continued his selfish behavior by telling Ann that she was irresponsible for socializing with the church members. He even suggested that she was not a Christian since she was spending too much time at the church and leaving him alone.

Buying her beautiful roses for Valentine's Day, was his way of showing her that he loved her. She thanked him for the flowers but continued to attend the church. One Sunday, she invited him to an ice cream social at the church. He came and had a good time; she talked about how loving he was to give her flowers on Valentine's Day. He met the deacon, who loved working on old cars. They had something in common. He asked him to attend a car show with him. He became less abusive; and thanked Ann for involving him at the church.

Ann joined a small group of women who were dealing with dangerous environments at home. She realized that she was dodging the harms and did not understand how to react to her sufferings. One technique she learned was to write just what Greg was saying that hurt her immediately after the incident.

The most important action was remembering how she felt at the time she was hurt. The question she asked in her prayers was, Would Jesus say this? She began to tell God about her understanding of the words. She also told Him about the place and time the words were said. Most of all was the visual expressions that she remembered Greg to resemble. Learning to talk to God by praying; remembering that God knows all about it and that He helped her before this event and will help her again. She also discovered that God does answer pray, believing that faith she will give her relief. This was tough for her because she sought a quick solution.

During the next group meeting, she shared her situation with the women. The important act was sharing her written words at the time of the abuse; and now with others whom she trusted. The group discussed Saint Paul's letter to the Thessalonians where he urged Christians to warn those who are unruly, comfort the fainthearted, uphold the weak, and be patient with all. The scripture also reads, "See that no one renders evil for evil to anyone, but always pursue what is good both for yourselves and for all." (1 Thessalonians 5:15). The next problem was, How does she warn Greg about his unruly behavior without harming herself?

Pursuing Good for All

She decided to think that time spent one-on-one would benefit the marriage. If the Holy Spirit is in both spouses with

Jesus Christ as the head of the family, God is with them. Ann prayed that she might feel safer with Greg; and the Lord gave her the insight to make a habit of carving out special moments solely for Greg. This time included communicating, developing better friendship, connecting emotionally, and sexual intimacy.

She started to set goals and make plans with Greg. Dan Seaborn and Peter Newhouse's research named "'Stay Married for Life'" suggested that time doesn't have to be spent outside the house, but it does have to focus on growing the relationship.

Ann began a discussion each day around exciting topics of gratefulness for the day that concerned the family. News about the church activities were always news to discuss. When she began multi-tasking over her work schedules; she asked for advice from Greg. With a smile, she asked for his advice on some of the details that took much of her time.

She participated in a neurological workshop about the workings of the brain. This was great because she remembered that the amygdala in her brain sounds an alarm that triggers the adrenal glands to release dopamine through the veins when she becomes overwhelmed. Training herself to slow down by counting to one hundred and breathing deep relieved much stress.

Prayer, meditation, and reading scriptures assisted in reduction of blood pressure. She found that smiling, laughing, or holding hands helped to develop friendship. Later, it became easier to talk about money issues, which sometimes caused stress. Each started to love what the other loved; which made it a joy. They found out that their commitment to each other was more important than anything. This increased their commit to Jesus Christ.

Why should fools have money in hand to buy wisdom, when they are not able to understand it? (Proverbs 17:1)

After increasing their commitment to Jesus Christ, they found contentment and less trouble as it related to money. Once the fear of the Lord led their marriage; contentment increased untouched by trouble. The habit, of reading the Word, became a constant habit, changing most of the impulsive desires of the flesh. Knowing that God owns everything was a constant reminder to the them. As they began to recognize that God gave each of them the strength and the skills to produce wealth; they began to feel the peace and joy in all their possessions. Realizing the fact that God wants all couples to be like Him, it became easier to know that He wants people to be content with what they have.

An idea hit Ann like a brick on a dark and stormy night. She thought that she should cry out to the Lord about her feelings surrounding the fact that she was not spending the time given to her by the Lord effectively. Praising God was a behavior that increased in the family's life. It was helpful after each member of the family began journaling each day because it increased their trust and faith in Jesus Christ.

"Now godliness with contentment is great gain.". (1 Timothy 6:6 NKJV)

They found that having food and clothing was enough because they brought nothing into this world, and it was certain they can could carry nothing out. They prayed that the family would not desire to be rich or fall into the temptation to love money and become greedy. Deciding on a less expensive home, was not an easy problem to solve. Now time had to be spent on understanding. Matthew 6:19-20.

Do not store up for yourselves treasures on earth, where moths and vermin destroy, and where thieves break in and steal. But store up for yourselves treasures in heaven, where moths and vermin do not destroy, and where thieves do not break in and steal. (Matthew 6:19-–20.)

Naivete was not a trait of Ann and Greg. Deception and dishonesty could not fool them into gullible decisions. Having a good relationship with Jesus, enabled them to stop any dishonest deceiver. They just refused to let darkness in their life. Get-rich-quick schemes were shut out immediately when suggested to them. They made a point of purchasing what was necessary. Money, to purchase luxury items, was saved over several months. They always prioritized their needs over any luxury item. They became mature emotionally and spiritually about their needs. They practiced the command in Proverbs 14:8.: "The wisdom of the prudent is to give thought to their ways, but the folly of fools is deception."

A few tensions that they encountered were neglecting unpaid bills, overextending the few investments that they had, and incurring credit card debt that remained at the high limit. They totally ignored savings accounts.

Anxiety Weighs Down the Heart.

A few months passed faster than they could imagine. They forgot about praying and following their plans. Insatiable thirst for more material things influenced their minds. Knowing that God was their Provider, they were convinced that they wanted more material wealth. Making more money encouraged their greed. Savings were depleted because they had an impulsive desire to buy more expensive items. Friends invited them to socials with others with the same greedy attitudes. They liked and wanted more invitations and gifts from wealthy friends. These were new friends who did not value the Christian values. The sin of idolatry tempted the family values.

Luke 12:15 warns the greedy., "Then he said to them, 'Watch out! Be on your guard against all kinds of greed; life does not consist in an abundance of possessions.'."

Ann prayed diligently now that she was aware of the sin. Placing trust in worldly wealth to meet her need for love and security was not what she desired. This temptation failed to satisfy her. She repented and decided never to look for security or love through money. She belonged to Christ Jesus, and He lived in her through the Holy Spirit.

In casual conversation with a trusted friend, Ann referred to herself as an idiot. The way that she said that sarcastic thought to her friend caused the friend to wonder whether Ann was a true Christian. Thinking hurtful thoughts about herself showed that she had deep wounds and scars that needed to be forgiven. Now, her tongue was untamable; she was destroying the distance between her and her Lord. Anger against self can destroy a relationship with the Almighty God. God hears disrespectful tones about ourselves. Being bitter toward self is just as bad as being hateful toward a neighbor. We are never justified in hating ourselves. These concerns must be left at the feet of Jesus because he as paid the price for our sins when he was nailed to the cross. Ann prayed that she would never devalue herself again. The Holy Spirit revealed that keeping a journal with kind words about her character would help in developing self-esteem.

Ann was tempted on the following day to purchase a new car while her present car was only two years old. *I do not want this old thing,* she thought. She talked about her feelings to every person who would listen to her. Her friends did not help by saying that it would be fun to have a Lexus automobile. They encouraged her to get excited about the idea by making her feel that it would be fun to ride in a new car. The situation moved into sin when she got excited. Her propensity for material things was sinful, needing forgiveness for the thought. Casual friends may not be positive role models when they tell you what you want to hear. Ads on the television were tempting, causing her to have an uncontrollable longing for sin. The Lord gives every believer rules on decision -making; requiring the believer to experience the consequences. When Ann drove to the nearest dealer, picked out the car, signed the papers, and drove away without negotiating on the transaction or consulting Greg; she needed to repent and live with this major problem.

As Greg was popping popcorn, he stared into space and became angry. He said that he could not understand what was causing Ann to be so impulsive about major purchases knowing that money was tight. She knew that the budget could not take this purchase. Repenting was one thing; but living above our budget was going to ruin their marriage. He prayed to the Lord and asked for Him to reveal to him what he should do. He decided to encourage Ann to return the car since they had just paid off a bill for golf clubs. The debt would soon destroy their marriage. They had a meeting where they established a range of prices for major purchases. They decided to check the internet in the future before making big purchases; and make calls to local stores.

Romans 15:7 tells us to accept one another, just as Christ accepted us. Greg and Ann were not commanded to agree with each other. They were commanded to love and look for ways to support each other. The marriage relationship means more than things or meaningless purchases. Praying to God and thanking the Him for the family relationship became a priority for both Ann and Greg.

After struggling with money issues for years, Ann and Greg started recognizing secret behaviors. Finding that suspicions about each other caused friction and hopelessness in their marriage. God revealed to them that frequent discussions about money matters helped in their positive journey of marriage. They started to act like they were dating once again. Learning to forgive was crucial for a long relationship. Once they stopped hurting each other with secrets while living in the same house; peace enforced the marriage. Blaming and defending each other could not be the answer if the journey was to continue. They found that distrust, rage, and suspicion disappeared; and their love and integrity for each other increased.

God promised in Psalm 37:4: "'Delight yourself in the LORD and he will give you the desires of your heart'." They found extreme satisfaction, great pleasure, and keen enjoyment in the Lord. Relishing time with the Lord meant loving and cherishing Him through their marriage. Living larger became a propensity for them to be controlled by the Holy Spirit.

Hard, Hardened Hannah
Distrusts God

Did Hannah fail to remember what Isaiah said in Isaiah 55:9? "For as the heavens are higher than the earth, So are My ways higher than your ways, And My thoughts than your thoughts." Those were words from the Lord God.

If we were to look into Hannah's thoughts, we would find a lack in her desire to trust others; therefore, she was missing out on intimacy with anyone, even God. Everyone that Hannah *encountered* loved her for her success. She desired favorable receptions from everyone at all times. If something went wrong, she would say that it was everybody's fault except hers. Hannah was so insensitive that she had no intimacy with her family.

Hannah was unforgiving toward everyone. She remembered Saint Paul's letter to the Colossians that commanded them to forgive as the Lord forgave them. (Colossians 3:13 NKJV). Hannah behaved as if she was the only person that was reliable, dependable, or trustworthy. Hannah learned to be fearful of intimacy. She learned at an early age how to snub people who wanted to soothe her.

At one time, Hannah had a problem, and her parents refused to help when she needed them the most. At that time, she began relying upon herself for comfort and affection. She had so much pain that she became greedy and selfish as if the whole world must bow down to her. She refused to turn to the Lord Jesus Christ as her safe haven.

Saint Paul's message to the Corinthians in 2 Corinthians 12:9 states that God's grace is sufficient for all believers of Jesus Christ. Telling God about her situations did not enter

Hannah's thoughts. She had no time to pray because she put her vocation as priority in her life. If only she could believe that God did not make us to be alone. Hannah was falling from God's grace; and it was hurting her relationships with others and God.

The Trials of Unforgiving Susan

Susan just does did not care anymore because she had been disappointed and left alone by close friends most of her life. Her proclivity attitude drove her into deep sin toward close friends.

"Whom have I in heaven but you? And earth has nothing I desire besides you." (Psalm 73:25)

If only, I can find a compassionate friend like Jesus; I would love and cherish Him.

She did not understand that knowing Jesus's kindness exceeds the joy and satisfaction of another human being. The desire to know the love of God deeper and understanding His ways more clearly could bring her closer to a spiritual companion. Dancing barefoot in her long nightgown, she o praised God and expressed her desire for the Lord to deliver. "Please, God," she cried, "I will never put You in a box to do what I desire; but to help me discern what You want me to do. I really am praying for a busy person to be my friend." Susan continually loved her relationship with the Lord; she knew in her heart that the Holy Spirit would send an angel to her.

Later in the year, her girlfriend invited her to join a small Bible study book club. The women started local social events, including men of faith. She mixed with people at work and the gym. She remembered the scripture "Make the most of every opportunity" (Colossians 4:5). Being pleasant with a smile when meeting others, was a characteristic that she displayed among strangers. She started to invite people to her home for socializing with her friends during holidays. Learning to ask questions to others was another quality of her sociability. Listening to others came easy to her once she learned to make "small talk". The Lord answered her prayer. She had more fun activities and made numerous friends who had countless interests that were similar to hers.

Susan found that refraining from applauding herself for her abilities helped her to gain more friends. She remembered scripture "Do not think of yourself more highly than you ought" (Romans 12:3).

"So in everything, do to others what you would have them do to you, for this sums up the Law and the Prophets". (Matthew 7:12).

Despite Susan's prayers, evil thoughts entered her mind. She had a proclivity for rich or exotic men. Thinking that she thought she was outstanding in modern dance, leading her to attract men especially when naked. Oh how she could get attention with her body. Immediately, she fell on her knees and prayed for forgiveness. *This was not the Lord's intent for me,* she thought. *A warm smile or a kind word to a friend was much better than, forcing my body on others.*

Becoming a weak person by developing a codependent relationship with another who thinks of himself as stronger caused Susan and many of her friends to have flawed friendships. Her failed friendships with people unable to share her interests and values caused her to pray and keep a journal about behaviors that just did not make sense. Sometimes people are unable to keep a job or do anything outside of themselves. A light bulb in her mind led her to wonder if someone was just having fun with her; never expecting to have a real relationship.

The Apostle Paul's letter to the church in Phillipi emphasized that the church should think about what is right and pure. If a friend was having consistent trouble paying bills or keeping a budget, Susan felt a need to ask if the person was irresponsible and prone to poor decision -making. King David's Psalm 37:21 states that the wicked borrow and do not repay.

Each day in her journaling led her to be strong in the Lord. She vowed, that another relationship with someone who seemed to see her as needy, was fruitless. Trusting in the Lord was the first step. She gained strength. Finding any friend required actions in a holy and honorable way. Passionate and lustful ways are not God's ways for Christians to gain friends. Her first friend was Jesus since He would never leave her.

Getting on her knees, she asked the Lord forgiveness in her intention to persuade others with perverted behavior. Her understanding as a Christian was the very thought of such behavior was sinful. After repenting, she began to learn new ways of communicating with other Christians. Feeling isolated and unimportant caused trauma. Coming closer to the Lord would require her to stand firm in her beliefs despite the secularly saturated society surrounding her everyday life.

Perverted, she applied power to accomplish wrong. Her "feel good" friends encouraged her evil ways. They would say to her "'come on, I am always on your side'." After learning to pray, she learned that real friends do not always agree with you. Real friends care her too much to pretend with her. She found that people lie often just to be near her. Once she stopped blaming others for her mistakes, she gained more truthful friends. Praying helps when there is a desire to be right. God will give the answer if you ask for His will to be done. Learning to wait on Him at His time is difficult when you are dishonest about her your intentions. God knows Susan's intentions before she had "'feel good'" friends'; and her intentions now and forever.

Susan's parents generally lied to her when she was young so that she would not have a temper tantrum. If her dress did not look good, she was flattered when told that it looked good. She heard and understood lies during her entire life. Her friends rarely encouraged or supported her in being truthful. She became lonely, especially when people ended their relationships with her because she was demanding, always getting upset if they did not agree with her.

Going to the Lord before asking wisdom on how to handle a situation from a friend who always agrees with you about everything really pays off. God never fails.

Lightning Source UK Ltd.
Milton Keynes UK
UKHW011843060921
390144UK00008B/511/J